For Jason ~ N.C.

International Standard Book Number: 978-1-56148-684-7

Library of Congress Catalog Card Number: 2009028319

Text and illustrations copyright © Natalie Chivers 2010
Original edition published in English by Little Tiger Press,
an imprint of Magi Publications, London, England, 2010.
Printed in China

Library of Congress Cataloging-in-Publication Data

Chivers, Natalie.
Rhino's great big itch! / Natalie Chivers.
p. cm.
Summary: Rhino has a terrible itch, and when Bird suggests he needs help
to scratch it Rhino sets out to find someone just right for the task.
ISBN 978-1-56148-684-7 (hardcover : alk. paper)
[1. Itching--Fiction. 2. Rhinoceroses--Fiction. 3. Birds--Fiction.
4. Jungle animals--Fiction.]   I. Title.
PZ7.C4456Rhi 2010
[E]--dc22
2009028319

Natalie Chivers

Rhino's Great BIG Itch!

Good Books

Intercourse, PA 17534
800/762-7171
www.GoodBooks.com

Rhino had an itch – a great
big terrible itch,
right in his ear.

He twisted . . .

he turned . . .

he wriggled,
he rolled.

But the itch just
wouldn't go.

"All you need is a little help," said Bird.

"You're right!" said Rhino. So . . .

. . . off he went to find someone
to scratch his itch.

"Can YOU scratch my itch, Frog?"
Rhino asked.

But Frog was
too slimy.

Monkey was too silly.

Lizard was too **prickly.**

And Rhino didn't even bother
to ask Lion!

It was no good.
The itch was still there.

"All I need is a little help,"
Rhino sighed.

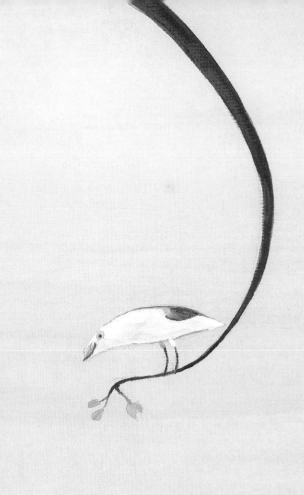

"I can help!"
said a little voice.

"How can **you** help, Bird?" asked Rhino.
"My itch is **big,** and you are far too tiny."

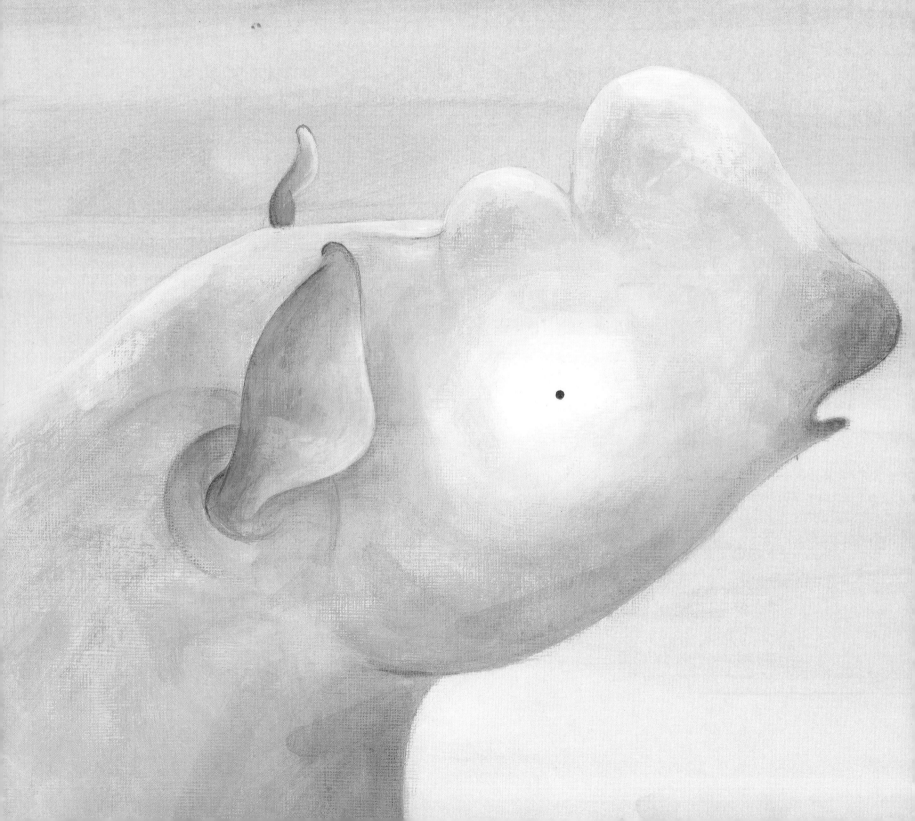

"I may be small," said Bird,
"but I am **just right** for you!"

So with
a hop . . .

and a skip . . .

and a little peck . . .

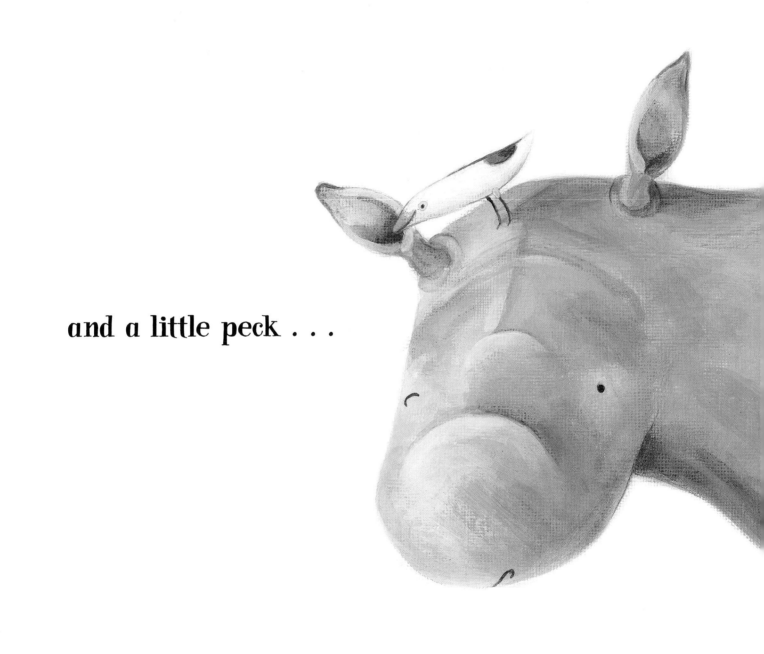

. . . the itch was gone!